*For Grandma Roz and
Granny Rose, who were all
about the spring, with love forever*
—S.B.

*For my mother, who also
needs a little help waking up!
All my love*
—P.C.

To Karen, Emma, and Dewey
—M.S.

Text copyright © 2000 by Samantha Berger and Pamela Chanko.
Illustrations copyright © 2000 by Melissa Sweet.
All rights reserved. Published by Scholastic Inc.
Printed in the U.S.A.

ISBN 0-439-45165-5

SCHOLASTIC, HELLO READER!, CARTWHEEL BOOKS, and associated logos and designs are trademarks and/or registered trademarks of Scholastic Inc.

16 17 18   40   11 12 13 14/0

It's SPRING!

by Samantha Berger
and Pamela Chanko

Illustrated by Melissa Sweet

SCHOLASTIC INC. Cartwheel BOOKS ®

New York   Toronto   London   Auckland   Sydney
Mexico City   New Delhi   Hong Kong   Buenos Aires

*I*n April the robin began to sing
to tell the rabbit it was spring.

The rabbit hopped and thumped his feet

to tell the deer the air smelled sweet.

The little deer ran with the bunny

to tell the duck the sky was sunny.

The duck swam off and gave a quack

to tell the cow, "The leaves are back!"

The cow let out a long moo

to tell the horse that flowers grew.

The horse went trotting down the lane

to tell the rooster, "Watch for rain!"

The rooster gave a mighty crow

to tell the mouse, "There's no more snow!"

The mouse just made a tiny peep

to tell the birds to start to cheep.

Then all the birds began to sing
to tell the bears, "Wake up, it's spring!"